Speed Demons

Adapted by Jasmine Jones

Based on the series created by Dan Povenmire & Jeff 'Swampy' Marsh

PaRragon

Bath • New York • Singapore • Hong Kong • Cologne • Delhi
Melbourne • Amsterdam • Johannesburg • Auckland • Shenzhen

This edition published by Parragon in 2011
Parragon
Queen Street House
4 Queen Street
Bath BA1 1HE, UK

ISBN 978-1-4075-8488-1
Printed in UK by CPI Boookmaque, Croydon

Part One

Chapter 1

Phineas Flynn and his stepbrother, Ferb Fletcher, had a problem. It was a beautiful summer day, and they had nothing to do.

Here they were just sitting under a tree with their pet platypus, Perry.

"So, Ferb, what should we do today?" Phineas asked. "I mean, besides giving Perry a bath." He leaned over to sniff his pet.

Ferb looked at Perry. The platypus made a

low clucking sound. Ferb didn't say anything in reply, which wasn't unusual. Ferb was the strong, silent type. Except that he wasn't particularly strong. He and his father were from England. Ferb's dad was married to Phineas's mum. Phineas and Ferb had been best friends from the moment they met. They thought of themselves as brothers, not stepbrothers.

Just then, a loud, zooming roar cut through the silent, summer breeze.

Ferb looked at Perry again, but Phineas was already peeking over the backyard fence.

A deafening buzz was coming from the other side. Phineas saw a huge motor speedway. Cars were zipping around the track. A brilliant idea popped into Phineas's brain. "Awesome!" he cried. "Ferb, I know what we're going to do today."

"Oh, I have got to take a new picture of myself for my blog." Phineas's older sister, Candace, frowned at the photo of herself on her mobile phone. "I didn't realize mine is already a week old." She pointed the camera at her face and snapped another picture. It looked exactly the same as the old one.

"That's better!" she said brightly as she

walked past the door to the garage.

Something strange was afoot in there.

Sparks flew. Smoke rose. Saws buzzed.

Candace stopped in her tracks. "What are you doing to Mum's car?" She glared at Phineas and Ferb. They were busy turning the family saloon into... something. It had a large number on the side and turbo boosters on the top.

Phineas and Ferb popped out of the roof. "We tricked it out," Phineas explained.

Candace rolled her eyes. "You don't even know how to drive!"

"Well, duh," Phineas shot back. "That's why Ferb built this remote."

Ferb held up the remote control and flipped a lever. The car's engine roared to life.

Candace narrowed her eyes. "Oh, you are so busted! Mum!" she shouted, darting through the house. "Mum! Mum!" Candace ran through every room. Her mother was nowhere to be found.

Candace finally ran back to the garage. "Um... where's Mum?" she asked.

Ferb was jumping on a giant engine, trying to force it under the bonnet of the family saloon.

"She's playing bridge at Mrs Garcia-Shapiro's," Phineas explained.

Candace hurried across the street. She couldn't wait to see the look on her mother's face when she saw the car.

Phineas and Ferb would be totally toasted. *Finally*. They always got away with everything. And Candace never got away with anything. Such as that time she borrowed her mum's sweater without asking. It wasn't even Candace's fault that Stacy had spilled grape juice on it! But, of course, Candace got in trouble anyway.

Now it was Phineas's and Ferb's turn.

"They won't get away with it this time!" Candace laughed as she rang Mrs Garcia-Shapiro's doorbell.

Mrs Garcia-Shapiro's round face lit up when she answered the door. "Oh, Candace, dear," she said in her slight Spanish accent. "What a coincidence. Do you know your mum is here?"

"Yeah, I do, Mrs Garcia-Shapiro." Candace smiled sweetly. "I need to talk to her if you don't mind."

"Oy, vey!" Mrs Garcia-Shapiro didn't move out of the doorway. "Look how tall you are now! You must have grown a couple of inches since the last time I saw you."

"That was last week, Mrs Garcia-Shapiro." Candace tried not to sound impatient. She

9

really wanted her mother to see what Phineas and Ferb were doing – before they got away with it! But Mrs Garcia-Shapiro loved to chat.

"Well, your mum's inside, dear," Mrs Garcia-Shapiro said. "Where are your braces? I thought you were wearing braces."

"Yeah," Candace said absently. A car zoomed down the street behind her. It was her mum's car! "Mum!" Candace shouted. "Mum! Mum!"

Linda Flynn-Fletcher didn't look up from her cards. She and the other members of the bridge club were all sitting at the table. They were in the middle of a hand. "What is it, Candace?"

"You have got to see what Phineas and Ferb are doing!" Candace looked across the street. The car was zipping back and forth behind her. Phineas and Ferb were on the front lawn, watching

it go. Ferb had the remote control. Their hair blew back every time the car whooshed past.

"Hey, Ferb," Phineas said, peering down at the remote. "What's the red button for?"

Ferb pressed the red button. Rockets appeared beneath the car.

"Mum!" Candace shrieked, just as the car shot into the air.

Linda hauled herself out of her chair. "What is it?" she asked. She walked over to Candace's side. "What do you want me to see?"

"Look!" Candace pointed across the street.

"Hi, Mum." Phineas said as he and Ferb smiled and waved. The car had disappeared.

"Hi, boys," Linda called. She looked down at Candace, whose mouth was hanging open. "Well, if that's all, I'll just be getting back to the game."

Linda turned and went back inside just as the car dropped from the sky, landing right in front of Phineas and Ferb.

"Good thing we reinforced the suspension," Phineas said.

Ferb flipped a lever and the car spun around in circles. It moved so fast, it looked like a tornado!

"Whoa!" Phineas said, his eyes wide. "What else can it do?"

"Hi, Phineas."

"Oh, hi, Isabella." Phineas turned to his friend, a pretty black-haired girl, who had just appeared beside him. She had on a pink dress and wore a pink bow in her hair.

"Whatcha doin'?" Isabella asked.

"We're entering the Swamp-Oil 500 today," Phineas explained. He pointed towards the racetrack.

Isabella thought for a moment. "Aren't you going to need a pit crew?" she asked.

Phineas lifted his eyebrows in surprise. Isabella was right – he did need someone to help change his tyres and fill up his petrol tank between laps. "Do you know a pit crew?"

"Well, I know a few people who work well together," Isabella said.

13

"Great, you're hired!" Phineas said happily. "See you at the track." He looked over at his brother. "Hey, Ferb, where's Perry?" he asked.

Ferb shrugged.

Phineas shook his head. This day was getting out of hand. He and Ferb had built a race car. They were about to enter the Swamp-Oil 500. And now their pet had disappeared!

Chapter 2

Perry the Platypus had an assignment. He pulled out his felt fedora and a remote control. He pressed a button, and a panel on the side of Phineas and Ferb's house slid back. Perry stepped inside. He dropped down a long tunnel and landed in his secret lair. He hurried to the control panel. A giant screen flickered to life. A military man with a serious face and a square jaw looked down at the platypus. Major Monogram was Perry's boss.

Perry the platypus worked for a secret branch of a secret branch of a secret part of the government. He was undercover. Even Phineas and Ferb didn't know his true identity. They thought Perry was just a pet. But the platypus was a secret agent.

"Good morning, Agent P," Major Monogram said.

A photo of a devious-looking man in a white lab coat appeared on the screen. "The evil Dr Doofenshmirtz is up to his old tricks,"

Major Monogram explained. "For reasons completely unknown, he's purchased a giant airship, or 'blimp,' as the kids say. Your mission is to find out why, and, if necessary, put a stop to it!"

Perry nodded. He had dealt with Dr Heinz Doofenshmirtz before. No doubt he was up to something horrible. But Perry wouldn't let him get away with it. The top of the mechanical tree in Phineas's backyard opened up, and Perry blasted out of his cave in a flying car.

The platypus was on the case!

17

* * *

"Hi, Phineas," Isabella chirped. They were in the centre of a racetrack in a stadium packed with the sounds of roaring engines and screaming fans. "I got your pit crew." She motioned to a group of girls. They all wore identical brown uniforms and brown berets. Isabella was the leader of the Fireside Girls troop. Whenever there was a task to be completed, she knew she could call on them. Fireside Girls were always prepared.

"Cool!" Phineas grinned. "See you in the pits!"

Isabella pulled out a diagram. It was a picture of the car's reworked engine. "Okay, girls," she said. "We're dealing with a four-hundred-and-twenty-six-cubic-inch, fully blown V-eight with hypo-lifters, radical cam and a limited slip differential."

The girls flipped open their Fireside Girl handbooks. Gretchen raised her hand. "Would that be electronically fuel-injected?" she asked.

Isabella nodded. She just knew that the Fireside Girls were going to make the best pit crew ever! This was going to be great!

"Phineas!" Candace screamed as she plodded through the stands at the racetrack. "Phineas! Phineas!" Her voice was even

more deafening than the engines on the track.

"Hey!" A guy in the stands glowered at Candace. "I can't hear the cars!"

"Hey, Candace!" a cute boy called out. "I didn't know you were a racing fan."

Candace's eyes went wide. That blonde hair! Those blue eyes! It was her crush, Jeremy! She hadn't expected to see him here. "Who, me?" she asked as she slipped into the chair beside his. "Oh, yeah, I'm a big fan of those... those, uh... uh..." Her mind went blank. She couldn't remember the word for the things that went around the track. "That red one is cute," she said, pointing to the race cars.

"Oh, that's Billy Ray Diggler's car," Jeremy said. "He's great!"

"Yeah, yeah, he's the best!" Candace gushed. She fluttered her eyelashes at Jeremy. "That Billy Roy."

"Billy Ray," Jeremy corrected.

"Billy Ray. I – I love it when he turns left..." Candace thought about that. Didn't the cars go in a circle? That meant they were always turning left. "... And then he turns left again... and then..." Her voice drifted off.

Just then, an announcer's voice blared through the speakers. "And in the third lane, newcomers Team Phineas!"

What? Candace looked up at the JumboTron. Sure enough, there was Phineas!

"And look!" the announcer went on. "He's already got his own screaming fans!"

The camera cut to Candace as she screamed, "Phineas!"

Phineas looked up at the JumboTron. His sister was on the screen, hollering her head off. "Hey, Candace is rooting for us!" Phineas said to Ferb.

Phineas wasn't the only one who had noticed. "Candace, you're on the big screen!" Jeremy exclaimed.

Candace looked up at the giant image of herself. Her face was hideously twisted as she screamed her brother's name again. "Phineas!" Candace cringed in embarrassment. Great. Forty thousand people – including her crush – were seeing this. Why couldn't they have blown up the cute photo she had taken for her blog?

"And your little brother's going to be on TV!" Jeremy went on.

"Phineas... on TV?" Candace repeated. Sure enough, Phineas was being interviewed in front of a TV camera. An idea popped into her mind. "TV! That's it! They are so busted! Can you wait right here for a second? Thanks."

Candace rushed off towards the pay phones. She had forgotten her mobile phone. Just when she needed it most! If she'd had it, she could have snapped a picture of Phineas while he was on the JumboTron. Just her luck.

Candace dropped a coin into the pay phone and punched in Mrs Garcia-Shapiro's phone number. Finally, Mrs Garcia-Shapiro answered. Candace asked to speak to her mother.

"What is it, Candace?" Linda asked when she got on the line. "I'm right in the middle of a three no-trump."

"Turn on the TV!" Candace cried. She had to shout to make her voice heard over the engines roaring in the background.

"All right, all right, Candace," her mother said as she walked into Mrs Garcia-Shapiro's living room. "This better be good." Several different remote controls sat on the table in front of her. Linda had to guess which one turned on the TV. Finally, she chose the largest. She picked it up and pressed a button.

Static appeared and hissed across the screen.

"Well?" Candace demanded. "Well, do you see it?"

"Just a second, honey," Linda said as she pressed another button. A DVD slid out of the player.

"Turn on the cable box first," Mrs Garcia-Shapiro called from the other room.

"Hmm, all right." Linda picked up another

remote and pressed a button. "Wait. Okay, that's not it. Um, is it this one? No, this is another phone." She then picked up another remote and pressed a button. Pop music blared as a result. "Oh, I turned on the stereo."

"Mum, hurry up!" Candace whined into the phone.

"Okay. Just a second!" Finally, the TV screen came to life.

"Are you embarrassed by flaking, itching, peeling?" asked an announcer.

Linda frowned. "Candace, this is a dandruff commercial. Is there something you're trying to tell me?"

Candace groaned. It would probably take her mother another three hours just to change the channel! She looked over her shoulder. The race was about to start.

Chapter 3

"Okay, Ferb," Phineas said over his walkie-talkie. He was behind the wheel of their souped-up family car. Engines revved around him, ready to start the race. "Are we good to go?"

Ferb gave his brother a thumbs-up. He was standing at the top of a tower at the

edge of the track. He would have a great view of the entire race.

"And, with the race about to start," the announcer said over the speakers, "there's the Doofenshmirtz Evil Incorporated blimp."

Dr Doofenshmirtz was so good at being evil that he had actually turned it into a business. His large blimp floated over the speedway. The Doofenshmirtz Evil Incorporated logo was in big letters across the side.

Perry steered his flying car towards the blimp at top speed. When he was next to it, the platypus jumped into the blimp through a window.

"Ah, Perry the Platypus!" Dr Doofenshmirtz grinned. "I'm glad you're here, actually. I was just getting ready to serve some platypus under glass!" He pulled a red lever, and a glass jar clamped down over the secret agent. Airholes were cut into the side so he could breathe. Perry pounded his tiny fist against the glass. He was trapped!

"You're just in time to witness my latest invention," the evil doctor said, rubbing his hands together. "My Deflatanator Ray! Which I will demonstrate by deflating all the tyres at the Jefferson County motor speedway. After which I will deflate everything in the tristate area!"

Perry narrowed his eyes in anger. If the evil doctor deflated all the tyres on the speedway, the cars would crash. People would be hurt – including Phineas!

Perry had to find a way to stop the evil doctor – before it was too late!

Candace stomped down to the edge of the racetrack. "Phineas, you are in big trouble, mister!" she shouted at the cars as they whizzed past. A blast of exhaust landed all over her. She was coated in grime. She trudged back to her seat.

Jeremy winced when he saw her. "Candace, you've got a little –"

"Smile!" A flashbulb popped. "Souvenir picture?" a photographer asked. He held out a photo. "Only a dollar!"

Candace screamed at the sight of herself covered in soot. But then another bulb popped – in her mind. She had an idea. A brilliant, perfect, sure-way-to-catch-Phineas-and-Ferb-in-the-act idea! "Wait a second!" She shook off the soot and exhaust residue and grabbed the camera.

"Hey!" the photographer shouted.

But Candace had already hurried away. "Now I've got you!" she growled, snapping a photo of Phineas behind the wheel as his

31

car raced past. It came out perfect.

"Hey, missy," the photographer said as Candace shoved the camera back into his hands. "Two pictures, two bucks!" He handed her the photo of her grimy self.

Candace dug into her pocket. "Oh, yeah, uh, I've only got a dollar, but, uh, I just want the one." She kept one photo and pressed the other one into his hand. "You can just tear that other one up, okay?" She smiled as she raced off towards Mrs Garcia-Shapiro's house. "I've got them now!"

"And pulling up fast on the inside lane, it's number forty-two, Team Phineas!" the announcer said.

"Hey, Ferb," Phineas said over his

walkie-talkie, "do you think we can get any more power? I mean, I know it's just a battery, but I was thinking... uh, Ferb? We're actually slowing down now." Number forty-two had just fallen into last place, right behind an antique car that was supposed to be part of a *Cars Are So Much Faster Now* demonstration at the end of the race. "Ferb? Hello?"

Suddenly, number forty-two shot forwards like a bullet! Wind whipped against Phineas's face, making his cheeks flap against his teeth. "Oh, yeah! Now that's what I'm talking about!"

Ferb nodded as he watched number forty-two shoot past the other cars on the track. He'd hooked up the remote control to a huge battery. It was large enough to power an entire city block.

"Hey, Ferb," Isabella said into a red phone, "we should bring Phineas in for a pit stop."

Ferb gave her a thumbs-up. The Fireside Girls put out the signal. Phineas's car screeched to a halt in the pit. "All right, Fireside Girls, let's move, move, move!" The girls darted around madly, changing tyres, pumping gas, checking oil, and testing the hydraulics.

"That helmet looks so manly," Isabella told

Phineas. She handed him a drink.

"Thanks," Phineas said as he slurped his drink.

"Hit it, Ferb!" Isabella cried. Ferb pressed the POWER button on the remote control, and the car took off. "I'm so proud of you, girls," Isabella said as the car roared away. "And the bow was a nice touch, Gretchen."

Gretchen smiled as the Fireside Girls admired the giant brown bow on top of car number forty-two. It flapped merrily in the breeze as Phineas rounded the track.

Dr Doofenshmirtz cackled. "Listen to those fools! How about a little demonstration of my deflationary prowess!" He pulled the lever on his giant Deflatanator Ray. A green beam shot towards the racetrack.

But it missed the racing cars. Instead, it headed into the stands!

"I got it!" called a guy in the stands as a beach ball bounced his way.

Zap!

The ball popped as the ray hit it.

Whoosh!

The ball flew out of the stands and landed on the windshield of a race car!

"Ahhh!" the driver yelled as his car hit a billboard post. With a creak and a groan, the billboard fell onto the track and right near Phineas's car!

Car number forty-two turned right, then left, then right. It zoomed around the billboard, then under it.

"The Team Phineas car is avoiding every obstacle!" the announcer cried. "It's like he can see the whole darn track at once!"

"Go, Phineas! Go! Go, Phineas!" Isabella and the Fireside Girls cheered from the pit.

Of course, Phineas couldn't see the whole track. But the person driving his car could! Ferb handled the remote control from his perch above the track.

"Oh, yeah!" Phineas crowed as he sped around the track.

But the other cars weren't so lucky. The billboard bent into the shape of a ramp. The other cars couldn't turn in time. They went up the ramp-shaped billboard and shot into the air. One by one, they crashed around Phineas. Luckily, none of the drivers were hurt.

Car number forty-two moved around each crash quickly and zoomed over the finish line. Team Phineas had won the race!

Chapter 4

Candace pedalled towards Mrs Garcia-Shapiro's house on her pink and purple bicycle. She raced through the front door and handed the photo to her mother. "Well, Mum? What do you think of this?"

Linda frowned. "You've looked better," she said.

"Huh?" Candace grabbed the photo. "What do you me – aah!" Candace screamed when

39

she saw the picture of herself covered in soot. A shocked-looking Jeremy was gaping at her in the background. She had grabbed the wrong photo!

And now Phineas was going to get away with everything – again!

Dr Doofenshmirtz's beady eyes gleamed as he peered down at the wreckage on the speedway. Look at what a single beach ball had done! "Already they fear me! Listen to their screams. Imagine the mayhem once my Deflatanator Ray is fully charged!" he cried. The doctor opened up his machine. Inside, a mouse raced madly on a hamster wheel. He was creating the power for the whole ray! "Run, run like the wind, my little indentured rodent, and I will give you some cheese." Dr Doofenshmirtz walked to the refrigerator and

peeked inside. "Heh, I know I have some around here somewhere."

Perry knew this was his chance. He pulled out his Secret Spy kit. EMERGENCY CHEESE, it read. He skipped the Muenster and Swiss and went straight for the most powerful stuff, 'stinky'. Quickly, he loaded it onto a Secret Spy cheese arrow and shot it through one of the glass jar's airholes.

The arrow sailed through the blimp and landed in the back of the evil doctor's pants.

"There used to be some Roquefort in the

back here," Dr Doofenshmirtz said as he moved things around in the fridge.

The scent of stinky cheese wafted over to the mouse. It smelled so tempting. The mouse climbed off his wheel and out of the ray gun. It wanted that cheese! The mouse skittered over and climbed up the doctor's leg.

"I don't – hmm? Ay-ay-ay!" Dr Doofenshmirtz let out a scream as the mouse wiggled around. "Ayyyyy...!"

The evil doctor's shrieks shattered Perry's

glass cage! The freed platypus raced towards Dr Doofenshmirtz. Once in range, Perry flicked his wide, flat tail and whacked the doctor in the face. "Ah!" Dr Doofenshmirtz staggered backward. He stumbled against the Deflatanator Ray. "Oof!" A green beam shot from the ray. It hit a giant mirror on the back of a truck. The beam reflected off of the mirror and shot back towards the blimp.

Pop!

Hiss!

"Hmm," Dr Doofenshmirtz said. "I suppose I should have seen that coming."

The blimp exploded like a giant balloon.

"But, Mum, you've got to believe me!" Candace wailed. Her mother sat calmly at the bridge table, looking at her cards. "Wait a minute! I bet it's still on TV!" Candace ran into Mrs Garcia-Shapiro's living room and picked up the remote.

"That's good, Candace," Linda said absently. "Go watch a little TV."

"And look at this amazing finish," the announcer said as car number forty-two raced past the chequered flag.

There was Phineas – behind the wheel!

"Mum!" Candace screeched. "Mum! Quick! Come q-q-q-q-quick!"

With a sigh, Linda got up from her bridge game. "All right, I'm coming."

Candace giggled eagerly. This was even better than the photo! Phineas was so busted  this time! There he was – and Ferb, too – accepting a giant gold trophy.

But suddenly, the camera cut to an image of a blimp. It was the Doofenshmirtz Evil Incorporated blimp, and it was losing air fast.

"Oh, no!" the announcer cried as the damaged airship sailed toward a tower. "A

blimp is about to hit the broadcasting tower! Oh, the –"

The picture disappeared from the screen as the tower fell. Static hissed from the television.

Linda walked up to Candace and gazed at the blank TV. "Uh-huh," she said. She gave her daughter an even look.

"Meep." Candace let out a squeak. It was all she could say.

Dr Doofenshmirtz's blimp was down. But that didn't mean he was going to give up! He jumped behind the wheel of the nearest race car – number forty-two.

Phineas, Ferb and the Fireside Girls watched as the car zoomed off.

"Hmm," Phineas said. "Looks like we're walking."

Suddenly, something landed on the hood of Dr Doofenshmirtz's car. It was Perry! And he had the car's remote control!

Chapter 5

"'Why don't you go back home, Candace?'" Candace muttered to herself, mimicking her mother's response to being pulled away from her bridge game yet again. Rolling her eyes, she heaved a sigh. "She has no idea." But at that very moment, Candace looked in the garage and saw something very interesting.

And that something was – nothing.
The family car was gone! *Of course!*
Candace gasped. "Gotcha!"

Dr Doofenshmirtz screamed as Perry steered the car through the streets. With a screech, they turned into a car wash. The doctor leaped out and tried to catch the platypus as water rained down on them.

A giant buffer whizzed overhead as it descended from the ceiling. Perry ducked, but the doctor was too slow. He got caught in the bristles of the enormous brush.

Perry sat on the hood of the car as he steered it out of the car wash. He was just deciding his next move when he accidentally stepped on the remote control's red button.

The car shot into the air like a rocket!

It soared high over the city and finally came to a landing... right in front of Phineas's and Ferb's house!

* * *

"Mum! Mum! Mum! Mum! Mum!" Candace was back, pounding on Mrs Garcia-Shapiro's front door.

"Oh, Candace," Mrs. Garcia-Shapiro said as she appeared at the door. "Hello. I can't believe you've grown so much. It's unbeliev-able –"

But Candace raced right past Mrs Garcia-Shapiro and into the dining room. "Mum! Mum, you've got to see this! It's about your car!"

Linda looked up from her cards. "All right," she said, finally giving in.

"Come on! Come on! Come on!" Candace said as she practically shoved her mother across the street.

"Candace, you're wearing out the heels of my shoes," Linda said.

Candace ran to the garage and flung open the door. "See, Mum? Look! Look! I told you!"

Linda gasped. "But... who did this?"

"Phineas and Ferb!" Candace crowed.

"You mean..."

Candace nodded eagerly. "Yeah! Yeah!

Yeah!" This was the moment she had been waiting for!

"They..."

"Uh-huh, uh-huh, uh-huh!"

"They washed my car?"

"Yes – ! No – ! What?" Candace blinked. There it was – the family saloon. The numbers and extra exhaust pipes had come off in the car wash. It was gleaming and looked perfect.

"It's beautiful!" Linda exclaimed.

Just then, Phineas and Ferb walked through the front door carrying a giant gold trophy.

"Hi, Mum," Phineas called. "We're home!"

Linda was still gazing at her clean car. "Hey, boys. I saw what you did today."

"Yeah?" Phineas asked as he and Ferb headed to their room to put away the trophy. "How'd you like it?"

"I loved it!" Linda bustled into the kitchen. "Now, who wants some snacks?"

"Thanks, Mum," Phineas said.

Linda looked over at Candace, who was still staring at the car. Her jaw had dropped open.

"Honey," Linda told her, "close your mouth."

But Candace couldn't believe it! Her brother was going to get away with borrowing the car and winning the Swamp-Oil 500!

Candace narrowed her eyes. This wasn't over. Not by a long shot.

Part Two

Chapter 1

It was another beautiful summer day. Phineas and Ferb were sitting under a tree in their backyard. "So, Ferb," Phineas said after a while, "what do you want to do today?"

Ferb shrugged.

"What about Perry, what does he want to do?" Phineas asked. He looked down at their pet platypus. Perry was sprawled on the grass with a blank look on his face.

The platypus made a low clucking sound.

"Well, he's a platypus," Phineas said, half to himself. "They don't do much." At least, Perry never *seemed* to do much. But Phineas couldn't just lie around all day. He liked to do things. And hanging out under a tree in the backyard wasn't cutting it. "I, for one, am starting to get bored, and boredom is something up with which I will not put."

Phineas leaped to his feet. "The first thing they're going to ask us when we get back to school is what we did over the summer! I mean, no school for three months. Our lives should be a roller coaster! And I mean a good roller coaster, not like that one we rode at the state fair."

Phineas shook his head. That state-fair roller coaster was pathetic. The car had clinked to the top of the incline and then dropped – about six feet.

"Man, that was lame." Phineas snorted in disgust. "Why, if I built a roller coaster I would..." Suddenly a brilliant idea popped into his mind. "That's it! I know what we're going to do today!"

"Phineas!" Linda called as she walked

into the backyard. "Ferb! I'm gonna go pick up a few things. You boys stay out of trouble, okay?"

"Okay, Mum," Phineas promised. After his mother left, Phineas turned to Ferb and exclaimed, "We're going to build a roller coaster!"

Candace peered out the window. Her mother was going out! That meant she was going to be alone with Phineas and Ferb. Candace hurried out to the driveway. "I'm in charge, right?" she demanded as her mother got into the car.

"Relax, Candace," Linda told her. "Nobody has to be in charge."

"But what if there's an emergency?" Candace demanded.

"Like what?"

"What, if, uh..." Candace racked her brain. There had to be some way for her to be in charge! "What if a satellite falls out of orbit and crashes into the house?"

"If that happens," Linda said, "you're in charge." She started the car and drove off.

"Yes!" Candace poked her head through the gate to the backyard. "Mum says I'm in charge," she told Phineas and Ferb. "Conditionally!"

Phineas didn't look up from the blueprints in front of him. "Whatever."

Ferb was beside him, working out some calculations. He and Phineas had set up a couple of tables for their project.

"Wait a minute, what are you doing?" Candace scowled at Phineas's drafting table. It had a picture of a weird, snaking, bridgelike thing on it.

"Homework," Phineas replied.

Candace frowned, suspicious. "It's summer!"

"That's cool," Phineas said in a bored voice.

"*You* wait till the last minute, then."

"Well, I'm watching you," Candace warned as she headed into the house. "And I'm in charge... conditionally!"

Just then, the phone rang. Candace picked it up and flopped into her favourite armchair. "Hello? Oh, hi, Stacy," she said, throwing her legs over the chair's arm. "No, I can't go to the mall right now. Mum just went to the store. She left me in charge. Well, you know, conditionally. Oh, if you go, can you see if Jeremy is there? No, no. He's the cute one that works at Mr Slushy Burger. Yeah, he totally smiled at me last time I was there. I just about died."

Candace turned her back to the glass-sliding door. That's why she didn't see Phineas and Ferb as they strolled through the backyard with a ton of roller coaster supplies. Actually, it was more like two tons. They had metal, rivets, wooden boards, concrete – even a few sinks.

"No, I told you," Candace babbled on with Stacy. She had no idea that anything unusual was going on behind her out in the yard. "I can't. I'm watching my brother and stepbrother." She propped herself onto the chair's back and twirled the phone cord around her finger. "Yeah, and they never get into trouble 'cause Mum never catches them." Candace turned upside down and kicked her legs in the air. "One of these days, though, I'm going to see to it that she catches them red-handed." On the other side of the glass door,

Phineas and Ferb walked by with a plastic pink flamingo and a caged lion. The lion let out an enormous roar.

Candace hopped off her chair and over to the sliding door. "Will you keep it down?" she screeched. "I am trying to use the phone!" She held the receiver back to her mouth as she fell back into the chair and dangled her legs over the arm. "Well, Mum left me in charge, so there'll be no shenanigans today. What are they doing right now? Why do you ask?" Candace sat straight up. "What do you mean you can see it from your house? See *what*?"

Candace rushed outside. "Phineas, what is this?" A giant metal structure stretched taller

than the backyard oak. It reached over the fence and into the neighbour's airspace.

Phineas smiled at her. "Do you like it?" he asked as Ferb fastened a board to a rail.

"Ooh, I'm gonna go tell Mum, and when she sees what you are doing, you are going down!" Candace cried. She raced to the garage.

Phineas turned to Ferb. "We're going to need a blowtorch and some more peanut butter." The blowtorch was for the roller coaster rails. The peanut butter was for lunch.

"Hey, Candace," Isabella said as she walked up the driveway. "Is Phineas..." But Candace was already zooming towards the supermarket on her pink and purple bicycle. "...home?" Isabella finished, mumbling to herself. Candace was long gone.

"Hey, Phineas," Isabella said as she walked into the backyard.

"Hey, Isabella." Phineas was studying the part of the roller coaster that was already built. He felt it needed something more. He searched through their box of supplies.

"Whatcha doin'?" Isabella asked. She looked up at the giant pile of metal.

"Building a roller coaster," Phineas explained.

"In your backyard?" Isabella asked.

Phineas shrugged. "Some of it."

"Wow! Isn't that kind of impossible?" Isabella asked. She thought Phineas was simply amazing.

Phineas smiled. "Some might say." Of course, Phineas knew that 'impossible' didn't exist. Not with a stepbrother like Ferb.

"Hey, Ferb!" Isabella called.

Ferb waved his hammer from his place at the top of the roller coaster.

"Does your stepbrother ever talk?" Isabella asked Phineas.

"Ferb?" Phineas asked. "He's more of a man of action."

Ferb hammered a nail.

"I was going to go to the pool," Isabella told Phineas. She dug her toe into the ground. "You want to go swimming?"

"Kind of in the middle of something here," he said and he pointed to the coaster.

"Oh, right." Isabella nodded. "Okay, I'll see you later then."

"Okay," Phineas said absently as Isabella trotted off. "Hey Ferb, you got enough rivets up there?"

Ferb shot four rivets into place. He blew on the rivet gun to cool it as the rail gleamed in the sun.

"Hey," Phineas said suddenly, "where's Perry?"

Chapter 2

Even if Phineas had known where Perry was, he probably wouldn't have recognized him. The platypus was now wearing his brown felt fedora. His blank expression had turned to one of grim determination. Perry had transformed into the brave and amazing Agent P.

Perry pressed the button that opened the secret panel on the side of Phineas and Ferb's house. He plunged into the tunnel that led

to his secret lair. As soon as he entered the cave, he noticed that the giant screen had just blinked to life – INCOMING MESSAGE, it read.

"Good morning, Agent P." Major Monogram's face stared down from the huge monitor. "The evil Dr Doofenshmirtz is up to his old tricks," he explained. "For reasons unknown to us, he has bought up eighty per cent of the country's tinfoil. I want you to get over to his hideout right away, find out what he's up to and put a stop to it!"

Perry nodded. He was eager to go after his old enemy, Dr Heinz Doofenshmirtz.

"As always, Agent P," Major Monogram

said, "it is imperative that your cover identity as a mindless domestic pet remains intact. Now, get out there, we're all counting on you!"

Perry gave one final salute. Then he raced to his flying Platypus Car. He leaped behind the steering wheel and blasted out of the cave. As he soared through the air, he flew right by Phineas and Ferb. Their roller coaster already stretched several stories into the air. Perry yanked his hat low over his face. He didn't want to blow his cover! Luckily, Phineas and Ferb were too busy working to notice their pet rocketing past them in a supersecret-spy airship.

"So, the way I see it," Phineas said to Ferb, "the solid-fuel rockets kick in in the mall car park, then we release the snakes during the corkscrew around the interstate. I'm gonna go get the snakes." Ferb flipped down a dark visor as Phineas started down the metal hill.

Ferb fired up the blowtorch. He had a lot of work to do.

"Mum!" Candace yelled out in the middle of the cereal aisle. Drippy music played in the background at the Super Food Stuff Mart. It was starting to get on Candace's last nerve. "You've got to come home right now!"

Linda pulled a box of cereal down from the shelf. "Did a satellite crash into the house?"

"No, no, no!" Candace cried. "You've got to see what Phineas and Ferb are doing." Honestly, sometimes she couldn't understand how her mother could move so slowly! If she would just race home right away, they could catch the boys in the act!

"Seems like we've had this conversation before." Linda didn't sound too interested. She pushed her trolley down the aisle.

Candace trotted after her mother. "What do you mean?" she demanded.

"I seem to recall you telling me that the boys were training monkeys to juggle bicycles," Linda said. She studied the label on the back of a box of granola. "And when I came home, there was a stunning lack of monkeys."

"I still don't know how they cleaned that up so fast," Candace grumbled.

Linda sighed. "So, what's the emergency this time?"

"They're building a roller coaster!" Candace shrieked.

"'Candace, seriously," Linda said patiently, "isn't Phineas a little young to be a roller coaster engineer?"

In fact, Linda wasn't the only one who was wondering that.

Phineas and Ferb's roller coaster had already stretched well into the city. Ferb was busy welding a rail to the outside wall of a factory. Phineas was chatting with the factory foreman, explaining their project. The foreman looked from the stack of papers to Phineas, and back again.

"Aren't you a little young to be a roller coaster engineer?" the foreman asked.

"Yes," Phineas replied. "Yes, I am."

The foreman waited for Phineas to say more. But Phineas just looked up at him. "Well, I must say I'm very impressed," the foreman said at last. He nodded at the papers.

"The forms all seem to be in order, although I've never seen them filled out in crayon before." He pointed to the machines behind him. "So, if there's anything I can get you – anything at all – just, uh, let me know."

Phineas looked at one of the robots. It was putting together a car – very quickly.

It gave Phineas an idea.

"Do you think we could borrow one of those gadgets?" Phineas asked.

Thirty-seven minutes later, Phineas and Ferb's roller coaster was humming along! The robot was planting pieces in the ground at lightning speed. "Now, this is the life!"

Phineas said. He and Ferb were riding with the robot as it built the roller coaster.

Perry flew towards a tall building at the centre of the city. It was the headquarters

of Doofenshmirtz Evil Incorporated. Perry jetted to the top floor's glass dome and leaped in through a window. The evil doctor was waiting for him.

"Ah, Perry the Platypus," Dr Doofenshmirtz cried. "What an unexpected surprise. And by 'unexpected' I mean completely expected!" He pressed a button, and four arms popped out of the walls. They grabbed Perry by the hands and feet. He banged his head against one of the arms. It was solid metal. Perry was trapped!

But the platypus wasn't worried. He knew he'd find a way out of the doctor's evil grip!

Dr Doofenshmirtz pointed to a large video screen, where New York City gleamed in the sun. Perry frowned. He didn't remember New York being quite so... bright.

"I, Dr Heinz Doofenshmirtz, have covered the entire eastern seaboard in tinfoil," the doctor explained. He pointed to a large

machine. "And when I put my giant magnet next to my ingenious Magnetism Magnifier, I will pull the east in a westerly direction, thereby reversing the rotation of the Earth."

Perry narrowed his eyes. Why would the doctor do this? he wondered. What could he possibly have to gain?

"You may well ask yourself, 'Why would he do this?'" Dr Doofenshmirtz said. "'What could he possibly have to gain?' Well, let me just answer that by saying I haven't really worked out all the bugs yet. I mean, you know, the tinfoil alone costs a lot."

But Perry was hardly listening. He had spotted a screw on the floor. Then he noticed rays from the Magnetism Magnifier near the ceiling.

Perry had a plan.

"But Mum, I'm telling you, they're building it, and it's huge!" Candace wailed.

Her mother wheeled the shopping trolley around a corner. Candace caught a flash of green hair and purple pants. The green-haired person had just stapled a flyer to a post that caught Candace's eye. "'Phineas and Ferb Present the Coolest Coaster Ever,'" Candace read. "'Now open'?" She darted after her mother, screaming, "Mum!"

Just then, a couple of kids walked past the flyer. "Phineas and Ferb got a roller coaster?" one of the kids asked. "You think we'll get a discount if we bring the flyer?"

"Maybe we'd better take it." His friend ripped the flyer from the post. The kids hurried off towards Phineas's backyard.

Candace dragged her mother over to the post. "Here, look, look, look, see? I told you I'm not crazy. I told you!"

"And you're not crazy because... ?" her mother asked, staring at the post. The flyer had disappeared!

Candace blinked at the post, then let out a scream.

"I see your point, Candace," Linda said. "No crazy person would scream at a post like that. I'll be in the dairy section if you want to come yell at some cheese or anything."

Candace had to keep herself from screaming again. She didn't understand why this always happened to her! With brothers like Phineas and Ferb, who *wouldn't* want to yell at a post?

Chapter 3

A crowd of kids streamed into the giant striped tent that Phineas and Ferb had set up in the backyard.

Once everyone was inside, Ferb walked up to the stage. He tapped the microphone. Then he stepped back to let Phineas do the talking.

The lights went out. Rock music blasted through the tent. A disco ball sent rings of light around the room.

"Ladies and gentlemen, boys and girls, children of all ages," Phineas announced. "May I present to you a spectacle most of the morning in the making." Ferb pulled a cord and the curtain

dropped. Phineas swept his hand towards the roller coaster behind him. It went up, up, up and then up, up, up some more.

The crowd let out an *oooh*.

"The Coolest... Coaster... Ever!" Phineas

cried. It reached high into the sky, then plunged, like a tidal wave. It swept over the freeway. It swirled around office buildings. It looped and zoomed and zigzagged through the city.

"So," Phineas said, "who wants to go first?"

Everyone raised a hand.

A moment later, the kids had piled into the coaster cars. Ferb was in the front car. He was next to Phineas, who was explaining how to use the seat belts. The coaster slowly clink, clink, clinked straight up. "To fasten, insert the tab into the metal buckle," Phineas said. He held up the buckle to demonstrate. "To release, just pull back on the –" The buckle fell out of his hands and plunged to the ground.

"Oops!" Phineas said. "Well, you get the picture. That's about it. Enjoy the ride."

The Coolest Coaster Ever paused for a moment at the top of the hill, and then plunged straight down! Everyone – everyone except Phineas and Ferb, that is – let out a scream!

"You all signed waivers, right?" Phineas called out. He was just kidding, of course. He knew that the roller coaster wasn't dangerous. Well, not *very* dangerous.

The kids screeched as the coaster looped around the freeway. As it whizzed through downtown, hundreds of snakes dropped from a barrel overhead.

"Relax," Phineas said. "They're just rubber!"

At that moment, the coaster dropped deep

into a mud pit. When it came out, everyone was covered in muck! Then the Coolest Coaster Ever zoomed through a car wash. The coaster – and the kids – came out the other side looking shiny and new. A worker buffed the front of the coaster with a white towel. He gave the signal, and the coaster took off!

It swept up a corkscrew turn around Doofenshmirtz Evil Incorporated's head-quarters.

"Hey, look!" Phineas cried as they headed into a sharp zigzag. "Here comes the ahh-ohh-ahh-ohh-ahh-ohh!"

"Ahh-ohh-ahh-ohh-ahh-ohh!" The kids screamed as they went over the zigzag.

And that was just the beginning.

Perry knew he didn't have a moment to lose.

Dr Doofenshmirtz was busy trying to explain how his evil plan might actually work. "When I really make all my money back," the doctor said, "I – I could buy a bunch of east-facing real estate –"

But the platypus wasn't listening. The metal

arms holding him in place were just loose enough. He managed to twist towards the screw on the floor. Perry gave it a whack with his wide tail and sent it flying across the room.

"And sell it," the doctor said, "at a – " He stopped talking as the screw sailed past his head. "Ha!" he shouted. "You missed!"

But Perry never missed. The screw clanged off of the control panel and sailed into the air. It soared into the path of the Magnetism Magnifier's rays and zinged back towards the doctor.

"Ow!" Dr Doofenshmirtz cried as the screw landed right on his big toe. "Ow, ow, ow, ow, ow!" He stumbled backward into a button labelled ARMS.

The clamps that held Perry released his arms and legs. Perry was free!

The platypus moved closer

87

and punched Dr Doofenshmirtz in the face.

"Ow!" But the doctor wouldn't be stopped. He yanked a lever. The glass dome overhead folded back. The doctor turned on the machine. Its ray shot towards the east coast! "Now you are too late!" Dr Doofenshmirtz hollered. "Quake in your boots and watch helplessly as the unimaginable electromagnetic forces pull the eastern seaboard, thereby reversing the rotation of the –"

Rrrrrrip!

The tinfoil peeled away from the buildings. The eastern seaboard stayed put.

"Well, that didn't work," the doctor observed. Then he noticed something else on his monitor. The tinfoil was still floating through the air towards the Magnetism Magnifier. "And now we have a two-ton ball of tinfoil travelling two hundred miles an hour directly at us!" He turned to Perry. "We must separate the magnet from the magnifier before it is too late!"

Perry yanked on the magnet. The doctor pulled on the magnifier.

But the magnetism was too strong! They couldn't separate them!

The ball of tinfoil barrelled closer.

"Now, I know I have that club card in here somewhere," Linda said as she rummaged around in her purse. The woman behind the register smiled patiently. "I always have it with me, but my purse is such a disaster area. You know how it is."

Candace could still barely keep from screaming. She knew that if they didn't get home soon, Phineas and Ferb would manage to make the roller coaster disappear.

Just then, she heard a distant scream. Candace rushed outside. There it was! The Coolest Coaster Ever zoomed through the car park right in front of the supermarket! And Phineas and Ferb were in the front car! Candace shouted as she darted back into the store. *"Mum!"*

She couldn't believe it. Phineas was about to be flame-grilled. Big-time.

Chapter 4

"It's no use!" Dr Doofenshmirtz wailed. "It's no use! We are doomed!"

But Perry stayed calm. All of his secret spy training kicked in. He spotted a helicopter buzzing overhead. Perry grabbed his rope gun and shot it at the helicopter. Then he tied the other end to the magnet. As the helicopter flew away, it took the giant magnet with it. Perry rode the magnet into the sky.

"You did it!" Dr Doofenshmirtz shouted as the magnet broke away from the magnifier. "You saved us, Perry the Platypus!"

There was only one problem. The giant ball of tinfoil was still hurtling towards the magnifier. And Dr Doofenshmirtz was standing right beside it! "Curse you, Perry the Platypus!" he shouted as the ball of foil smacked into the top of Doofenshmirtz Evil Incorporated headquarters. The doctor, the corporation's top floor, and the tinfoil sailed across the city.

Meanwhile, many miles below, Candace was dragging her mother out of the supermarket. "Look, look, look!" Candace pointed towards the freeway. "See?"

Linda squinted into the distance. "Okay, I give up," she said at last. "What am I supposed to be looking at?"

Candace turned towards where the roller coaster was supposed to be. But now it was just empty air! She gasped. "No, it's not possible!"

"I'm going to go get the trolley." Linda walked off.

"It was right here," Candace insisted.

"Time to go," Linda said as she pushed the trolley towards the car. "I've got frozen food."

But Candace couldn't let her brother and stepbrother off so easily. "Okay, so you think that Phineas and Ferb are still under that stupid tree in the backyard, right?"

"Well, yes, that would be my guess," Linda said.

"Fine, then let's go home now!" Candace exclaimed as she hopped in the car.

Candace grinned as they neared the edge of their neighbourhood. This was it. Phineas and Ferb were finally going to get caught!

But what had happened to the roller coaster?

While Candace and her mum had been finishing their grocery shopping, Perry and the giant magnet had dangled over the city. When the tinfoil crashed into Dr Doofenshmirtz's building, it knocked loose the magnifier. The magnifier then had sailed through the air – and landed back on the magnet!

Now the superstrong magnet ray was pointing down toward the city. It immediately attached itself to the large metal structure directly below it – the Coolest Coaster Ever.

The helicopter began to spew black smoke as it hauled the giant coaster into the air. Perry pulled out a blade and cut the rope that held the magnet and the helicopter together. The helicopter flew off, and Perry dropped towards the ground, landing in one of the coaster cars as it zoomed beneath him.

"Oh, there you are, Perry," Phineas said as he noticed his pet two cars behind him.

Perry made a low clucking sound.

The kids screamed as the coaster rolled off the rails and up a busy street.

"Funny," Phineas said, "I don't remember this in the blueprints."

The coaster zoomed towards a crane and went around, around and around! It zipped into the air like a slingshot! "And I'm sure this is new," Phineas said.

The kids screamed again as the coaster sailed towards the eastern seaboard. It slammed against the Statue of Liberty's torch in New York Harbour. The statue bent backward, then rebounded. Next it shot the cars west. They sailed towards Mount Rushmore in South Dakota. They did a loop-de-loop around Teddy Roosevelt's glasses and flew into the air back towards Phineas's town. The coaster landed on a pine tree near the mall. The tree bent towards the ground.

"Welcome to Mr Slushy Burger," Jeremy said as the coaster paused near his stand. "May I take your order?"

"Anyone want fries?" Phineas asked.

But just then, the tree sprang back. The kids screeched as the coaster flew across the ocean. It landed at the top of the Eiffel Tower in Paris, which bent towards the street.

A guy behind the counter of a French cafe eyed the kids in the roller coaster cars. "*Croissant?*" he asked.

"Anyone want a *croissant?*" Phineas asked in a French accent.

But before anyone could answer, the Eiffel Tower shot backwards. It flung them higher and higher and higher. They went past the clouds and past the planes. They went right

into space and floated there for a moment.

A satellite beeped past.

"You know," Phineas said, "if that thing crashes to Earth, Candace is in charge."

Ferb blinked.

And then the coaster dropped.

"Ahhh!" The kids screeched as the Coolest Coaster Ever plunged towards Earth. Flames burst from the front car as they re-entered the atmosphere.

"We should've charged more," Phineas said to Ferb.

After all, this ride was *way* cooler than either of them had planned.

Chapter 5

"Okay, we're here," Linda said as she pulled into the driveway. "Are you happy now, Candace?"

Candace giggled as she hopped out of the car. Oh, she was happy. But not as happy as she would be when her brothers got busted! She yanked open the gate. The backyard was empty. "Yes! See, Mum? I told you they weren't there."

Candace heard a slight rustle in the tree behind her. Linda peered over Candace's shoulder. "Oh, hi, boys," Linda said.

Candace turned around to see... Phineas! And Ferb! Even Perry was there. All three were stretched out beneath the tree just as they'd been when Linda had left for the store.

"Hi, Mum," Phineas said.

"Come on, Candace, help me with the groceries," Linda said as she started back towards the car.

"Uh, but, but, but, but..." Candace stammered. Where was the roller coaster? Where were all the kids who were riding on it?

"Let's go," her mother said.

"But, but, but, but..." Finally, Candace gave up and trailed after her mother. Her brothers had somehow managed to get away with something impossible – *again*.

"Hey, Phineas," said one of the kids from the coaster, who dropped from the branches above Ferb's head a second after Candace departed. "That was great!" The roller coaster had come to a fiery stop in Phineas's backyard tree.

"Way too cool!" another of Phineas's friends agreed.

"That was awesome!" said another boy who descended out of the tree. "Can we do it again?"

The rest of the kids climbed out of the tree. Everyone looked eagerly at Phineas and Ferb.

"Sorry," Phineas told them. "Only one ride per customer."

"That was great, Phineas." Isabella smiled at him. "So what are you going to do tomorrow?"

"Don't know yet," Phineas said.

"Maybe you can teach Perry some tricks," Isabella suggested. She petted the platypus.

"See you tomorrow." Isabella waved as she trotted towards the gate. "It really was the coolest coaster ever. You guys make a great team."

"Well, a brother is a brother," Phineas said. "But I couldn't have asked for a better one than Ferb." He smiled at Ferb.

"So, what should we do tomorrow?" Phineas asked Ferb. "There's a world of possibilities. Maybe we should make a list."

Just then, the tree above them burst into flames.

105

"Mum!" Candace shouted as she watched from the window.

"Give it a rest, Candace!" Linda told her daughter.

Phineas looked up at the tree and smiled. The Coolest Coaster Ever had really rocked. It was turning into a pretty awesome week.

And the summer was just getting started...

Don't miss the fun in the next
Phineas & Ferb book...

RUNAWAY HIT

Adapted by Lara Bergen
Based on the series created by Dan Povenmire & Jeff "Swampy" Marsh

It was the start of another potentially boring summer day in the lives of Phineas and Ferb. As they ate their breakfast, a painfully bad *Super American Pop Teen Idol Star* contestant was croaking out a song on the kitchen TV. Phineas and Ferb listened as they dug into their second bowls of Sugar POWs and their mum, Linda, helped herself to her fourth cup of coffee. Phineas's sister (and Ferb's stepsister), Candace, was searching in the refrigerator.

"*I... met my love in a –*" the boy on the show belted out at the top of his lungs, sounding a lot like a human bagpipe, only worse.

As the boys watched, a big boxing glove shot out of nowhere and – *BOOM!* – whacked the contestant off the stage.

"Oh, boy!" cried the announcer. "Did that kid stink or what? Ha!" He laughed and shook his head, then grinned and pointed at the camera. "But maybe *you've* got what it takes to be..." as he spoke, the words flashed onto the screen: "... the next... *Super... American... Pop... Teen... Idol... Star*!! Auditions open today at the Googolplex Mall in beautiful downtown Danville!"

Candace immediately gave up her search for a raspberry yoghurt and ran to the TV. "Auditions! Today!" Her heart was pounding in her chest. Was it possible? Was her favourite show really having auditions at the local mall?

"Yes!" said the announcer cheerfully. "Today! At two o'clock sharp!"

"*Yes!*" Candace lifted the TV off the counter and planted a big wet kiss in the middle of the screen. "*Mwaahh!* I've got to tell Stacy!" She dashed off to her room to call her best friend right away. After all, opportunities like this didn't just up and land in a girl's very own hometown every day!

Unfortunately, Candace forgot that she was still holding the television set. And it was still plugged into the wall....

"Oh!" she cried, as her arms flew back and – THONK! – her rear end hit the floor.

Phineas and Ferb glanced at Candace from their seats at the kitchen table to see what all the noise was about. Then they went back to eating their cereal.

"That pop-star stuff might be fun at first," said Phineas between spoonfuls. "But then you'd be stuck in a dead-end job. Too bad you can't just do it once and move on."

"Well, what you're talking about," said Linda, taking another sip of coffee, "is a one-hit wonder." She walked over to the counter and stood next to the TV.

"A one-hit wonder?" said Phineas, looking up. "Ferb," he said excitedly. "I know what we're going to do today!"

Read *Runaway Hit* to find
out what happens next!